Marshal Monkey
and the
Banana Bandits

ISBN 978-1-0980-4422-0 (paperback)
ISBN 978-1-0980-4423-7 (digital)

Christian Faith Publishing, Inc.
832 Park Avenue
Meadville, PA 16335
www.christianfaithpublishing.com

Printed in the United States of America

Marshal Monkey
and the
Banana Bandits

Jeff Allen

It was a lazy afternoon in the town of Bed Springs. Marshal Monkey and Deputy Dillo were sitting in the marshal's office relaxing and enjoying a snack of fresh bananas from one of the local banana ranches.

"It sure has been quiet lately, Marshal," said Deputy Dillo around a mouthful of banana.

"Now why would you go and jinx us like that, Dillo? I ain't complainin' about the lack of criminal shenanigans. If it weren't quiet, we wouldn't be able to sit here and enjoy these here bananas right off the ranch."

Dillo swallowed his banana and replied, "Now I ain't tryin' to wish for trouble, Marshal, but it's usually busier than this."

"And all I'm sayin' is that you need to be careful what you wish for, Dillo."

Right then the front door burst open, and a man rushed in.

"Marshal! My bananas have been rustled!"

Marshal Monkey recognized the man as Beau Vine, a local banana rancher.

"Now, calm down, Beau, and tell me what you're talkin' about," said Marshal Monkey as he cast a look at Deputy Dillo.

"All right, Marshal. I got up this mornin' and went out to check the bananas, and they were all gone! Not one left anywhere. I saw some footprints leading away from the corrals, and I followed 'em to the river, but they disappeared."

Marshal Monkey looked at Dillo and said, "I told ya you were askin' for trouble by sayin' it was so quiet. Let's get saddled up and follow Beau back to his spread and look at the crime scene for clues."

So the marshal and Deputy Dillo got their horses saddled up and followed Beau Vine back to his ranch, The Peel Deal Ranch. Once they arrived, Monkey and Dillo began their investigation of the corrals.

"Marshal," said Dillo, "come take a look at this. It looks like a small piece of some other kind of fruit is lyin' here in among the tracks."

Monkey walked over and squinted at the piece of fruit. He took it from the deputy and sniffed it. "This smells like kiwi. Beau, are there any kiwi ranches around here?"

"Not anywhere hereabouts that I know of."

"Hmmm. That might mean that our bandits are moving around stealing fruit and then moving on before they can get caught. Let's follow these tracks and see if we can find any other clues. Dillo, how many sets of footprints do you see?"

"Ummm, while it looks like the tracks are all the same, Marshal, three different bandits made all of these because the shapes are all same but the sizes are different."

"That's what it looks like to me too, Dillo. Let's head down to the river and take a look-see."

Marshal Monkey and Deputy Dillo followed the tracks down to the river where they disappeared at the water's edge.

"Well, Dillo, it looks like our thieves are smart and took all the bananas up or downriver without crossing over the river. These bandits are good, I'll give 'em that, but we're better. They picked the wrong town to steal fruit. Let's head back into town and see if we can turn up any leads there." Monkey turned to Beau and said, "We'll get to the bottom of this, Beau. Don't you worry."

"I just want my bananas back, Marshal."

Back in town, Monkey and Dillo headed to The Cups Up Saloon, the local juice bar.

"If anything unusual's going on in town, or if anyone suspicious is in town, Walter would know," said Marshal Monkey.

Walter Ringhole was the proprietor and bartender of The Cups Up Saloon and had been in town longer than most of the other residents. As they walked into The Cup, heads turned to look at them, but realizing it was just the marshal and his trusty deputy, the patrons quickly went back to their juices. Marshal Monkey noticed a few unfamiliar faces scattered around the juice bar as he approached the counter.

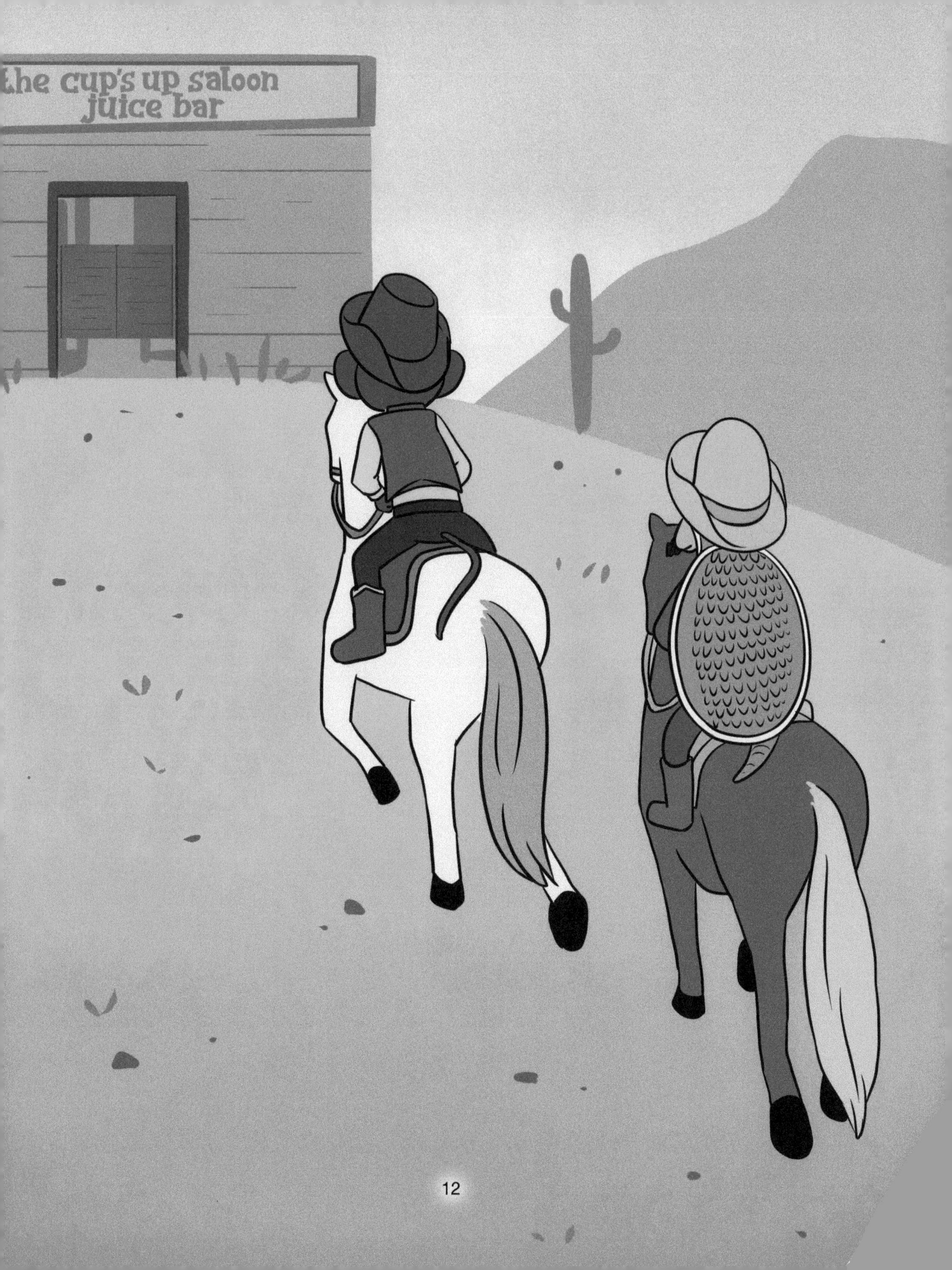
the cup's up saloon
juice bar

"Howdy, Walt."

"Afternoon, Marshal. What can I get ya?" asked Walt.

"Got any interesting juice today?"

"Well, I did just buy a wagon full of kiwi from these three fellers I ain't seen around town before. They didn't say where they was from, and I didn't ask 'em. I was just surprised I was able to get some kiwi. Ain't had kiwi here for a while."

"Those fellers still in here by any chance?" asked the marshal as he surveyed the room.

"Naw, they had a juice and then lit out, but that was this morning. I did hear one of 'em mention Tooda Point as they was leavin' though."

Dillo said, "Marshal, the Crimea River runs past Tooda Point. Maybe the banana bandits had a boat they sailed down the river, and maybe their camp is down at Tooda Point."

"You might be onto something, Dillo," said the marshal as he tipped his juice back. "Let's you and me go fishing down by the Point and see what we can catch. Thanks for the juice and the information, Walt."

"Anytime, Marshal."

Marshal Monkey and Dillo made their way out to the area of Tooda Point. They tied up their horses and started scouting around. Soon they heard voices ahead by the bank of the river.

"I told ya we'd do good for ourselves in this territory, lots of fruit to be had. Those bananas were just the start. And having a juice bar to sell the fruit too is almost too good to be true," said one voice.

"Yup, you shore did, Hampton," replied another. "But how long we gonna stay here?"

"As long as we can. I already have some ideas about our next job. Once we make enough, we can skedaddle back home," said the voice identified as Hampton.

A third voice chimed in, "Hey, Frampton, can you pass me another banana?"

This was all the proof the marshal needed. He motioned to Dillo, and they both jumped out onto the sandy bank, where they saw three little pigs around a campfire eating grilled bananas. Behind them, a large boat loaded with various fruits was aground on the shore.

The pigs began to stand up, and Marshal Monkey firmly stated, "Keep yer seats, gentlemen. I'm Marshal Monkey and this here"— pointing to Deputy Dillo—"is my deputy. We need to talk to y'all about some fruit rustlin' that happened."

The biggest of the three pigs said, "We don't know what yertalkin' about, lawman. We ain't done no rustlin' o' no fruit."

Marshal Monkey replied, "I'm guessing you're Hampton, the boss o' this here gang. We just heard you talkin', and you admitted you stole the bananas."

"Where we come from, you can take what you want, when you wants. Ain't no crime," said the one called Frampton.

"Well, Frampton, was it? Here in this territory, we operate under the Governor's Book of the Law. And it says in chapter 2, section 8 that stealing is against the law. Now, maybe you boys could steal things back wherever you're from, and that's fine, but the governor don't like crime. He hates it, in fact. Seein's how I'm the marshal, it's my duty to enforce the law. Is there anything you'd like to say before I put y'all in jail?"

The third little pig said, "We wasn't tryin' to hurt nobody, Marshal. We was just takin' fruit and sellin' it to make money for our ma. There's a Mr. Wolfgang keeps botherin' her and has knocked her house down twice. We ain't got no lawmen where we's from, or they might stop Mr. Wolfgang. We just wanna help her rebuild her house, but this time with brick. But brick is expensive, and we didn't have no other way to make enough money. Honest."

"Don't be tellin' him our family business, Chancho!" said Frampton.

Dillo asked, "Is this true? Your ma's in a bind?"

Hampton and Frampton reluctantly nodded in agreement.

Dillo leaned into the marshal and whispered, "Marshal, I know they broke the law, but it also says in the governor's law book that we're supposed to love our neighbors and be forgiving because the governor forgives us. Besides, these fellers were just trying to help their ma."

"I know, Dillo," whispered the marshal back. "And given their circumstances, I have an idea about how to dispense the right kind of justice. They need to pay for their crimes, but we also need to show some mercy." Looking at the three little pigs, Marshal Monkey said, "You boys come along now so we can get you to jail."

Later that week, Beau Vine entered the marshal's office again.

"Good to see you again, Beau. Hope all is well at the ranch. How're your new hands working out?"

"Well, Marshal, I had my doubts, but them three little pigs do seem to be working out. And they already know a lot about fruit and ranchin', so I haven't had to show 'em a whole lot. How did you ever think to have 'em come work for me?"

"Well, Dillo's the one who gave me the idea and reminded me we need to show 'em some mercy. By working for you, they get an honest day's work, get to make amends with you, get to make some money for their ma, and now the extra hands will let you expand your operation—somethin' you've always wanted."

"I have, indeed, Marshal. Thanks again for doing the governor's work."

"Anytime, Beau. Now if you'll excuse us, the deputy and I were headed over to The Cups Up to enjoy some guava juice. You're welcome to join us if you'd like."

"Don't mind if I do, Marshal, don't mind if I do," Beau said as they all walked out the door.

About the Author

Jeff was Saved back in 2007 after decades as the prodigal son. The only thing he regrets about being Saved is that it took him so long to come to the truth. Jeff is originally from east-central Ohio but, after gallivanting across the globe with the US Air Force in his job as Security Forces {the USAF version of military police}, now lives in northeast Utah. He's been to 11 foreign countries and is a veteran of Desert Shield/Desert Storm and Operation Iraqi Freedom. Jeff finally retired in 2015. Luckily, this area of Utah is dinosaur central which is perfect for his 10 year-old son who has wanted to be a paleontologist when he grows up since he was 6. Jeff got remarried earlier this year to his next door neighbor. He also picked up 5 step-kids in the merger, along with some sundry animals. Some of Jeff's hobbies and interests include hiking and enjoying God's creation, carpentry, reading, writing, movies, music, cooking, playing games with the family, hanging out with the kids, und lerne Deutsch langsam. Defensor Fortis!